PILGRIM CAT

Carol Antoinette Peacock

Illustrated by **Doris Ettlinger**

Albert Whitman & Company, Morton Grove, Illinois

To my family: Tom, Jonathan, Elizabeth, Katherine, our dog, Pepper,
and, of course, all our cats!—C.A.P.

In memory of my father, Carlton Ettlinger.—D.E.

I am grateful to the staff at Plimoth Plantation, Plymouth, Massachusetts, especially
Carolyn Freeman Travers, Research Manager, who graciously lent her expertise, and Rachael Walsh,
the Pilgrim guide who introduced my daughters to the present-day cat that inspired this story.
And heartfelt thanks to my editor, Abby Levine. Her ideas and steadfast support made this project possible.—C.A.P.

Library of Congress Cataloging-in-Publication Data

Peacock, Carol Antoinette.
Pilgrim cat / by Carol Antoinette Peacock; illustrated by Doris Ettlinger.
p. cm.
Summary: A young Pilgrim girl and the cat she discovers on the *Mayflower* voyage begin their life together in the Plymouth settlement.
ISBN 0-8075-6532-6 (hardcover)
1. Pilgrims (New Plymouth Colony) – Juvenile fiction. 2. Plymouth (Mass.) – History – Juvenile fiction.
[1. Pilgrims (New Plymouth Colony) – Fiction. 2. Plymouth (Mass.) – History – 17th century – Fiction. 3. *Mayflower* (Ship) – Fiction. 4. Cats – Fiction.]
I. Ettlinger, Doris, ill. II. Title. PZ7.P3117Pi 2004 [Fic] – dc22 2003026209

Text copyright © 2004 by Carol Antoinette Peacock. Illustrations copyright © 2004 by Doris Ettlinger.
Published in 2004 by Albert Whitman & Company, 6340 Oakton Street, Morton Grove, Illinois 60053-2723.
Published simultaneously in Canada by Fitzhenry & Whiteside, Markham, Ontario.
Printed in China through Colorcraft Ltd., Hong Kong.
10 9 8 7 6 5 4 3 2 1

The design is by Carol Gildar and Doris Ettlinger.

For more information about Albert Whitman & Company, please visit our web site at www.albertwhitman.com.

My daughters discovered a cat playing at Plimoth Plantation, the wonderful living history museum of Pilgrim life in Plymouth, Massachusetts. Did cats come on the *Mayflower*, too, I wondered.

From my research, I learned that cats sailed with the Pilgrims to the New World. Here is the imagined story of one of them, a cat named Pounce.

Pounce's mistress, Faith Barrett, is based on the lives of real Pilgrim girls. There were eleven girls on the voyage, ranging in age from less than a year to sixteen or seventeen.

Squanto, who befriends Faith in this story, was a Wampanoag Native who lived with the Pilgrims during the first trying years. Without his help, the settlers might have perished. Squanto taught the Pilgrims, adults and children, skills they needed to survive in this new place.

Two brief accounts, written by the Pilgrims themselves, are all we know about what we now call the first Thanksgiving, which took place in the fall of 1621. Some scholars believe that rather than being invited to a harvest celebration, ninety Wampanoag and their leader, Chief Massasoit, arrived because they were alarmed by the sound of Pilgrims shooting wild fowl. Then they stayed to feast. We know that the gathering included games, shooting matches, and dancing and lasted for three days.

The Wampanoag often gave thanks for the Creator's bounty, both at ceremonies and in daily life. While there is no specific record in the Pilgrim accounts of a prayer given by their Native guests at the feast, it is possible that gratitude was formally expressed.

C.A.P.

On a breezy September morning in 1620, a stray cat prowled the docks, hunting his breakfast. The cat spied a plump mouse. He pounced and missed. When the mouse escaped to a ship, the cat followed, landing on the ship's deck. The ship was called the *Mayflower*.

"A *cat* just jumped on our boat, Father!" Faith Barrett exclaimed as she waited with her family and the other passengers to sail.

"Every ship needs a few good mousers," said her father. "He'll catch the mice on board."

It was time to depart.

"Good-bye, England!" called Faith as the *Mayflower* set sail. The passengers were headed across the Atlantic, leaving all they loved behind. Faith's family and many others aboard were sailing to the New World so they could worship as they pleased.

At first, the weather was calm. Then the autumn storms came. One day the *Mayflower* began to pitch and roll. Faith's stomach reeled. She reached for a bucket and got sick.

Afterwards, Faith peered through the wooden grating over the "hold," where the food was stored. She looked down.

"The mouser!" she exclaimed.

The hungry cat was stalking a rat. Faith found some hard cheese that she had saved from supper and dropped it below. The cat batted the morsel with his paw. Then he pounced.

"I shall name thee 'Pounce,' " she said.

After that, Faith looked for him, hunting alone or playing with the other cats. Every day, she fed him a piece of dried meat or fish from her own meal. Pounce began to wait for her.

When the storms had passed, families were allowed to go on deck. How good it was to breathe fresh air! Throwing back her head, Faith twirled around and around. Then, dizzy, she looked at her feet.

"Pounce!" Faith said.

His eyes closed, his tiny face tilted upward, the cat was sunning himself nearby.

Faith scooped up the cat and brought him inside the ship.

"Thou art a beauty indeed!" she marveled.

Pounce purred.

"Oh, Pounce," said Faith, as she stroked his head. "This voyage is a trial! We are cold and so wet, even our blankets are soaked. We eat moldy cheese and biscuits filled with worms. And then the storms! I do fear we will perish at sea and never reach the New World."

For the rest of the voyage, Faith and Pounce were always together. Faith sang him all the songs she knew. She told him riddles and made up stories for him. At bedtime, Pounce slept on Faith's chest while the *Mayflower* swayed through the night.

Then, after sixty-six days, the crew heard birds!

Pounce sat, alert. He heard them, too.

Leaves floated by in the water. "Land, ho!" shouted the sailors.

On December 16, 1620, the *Mayflower* sailed into a sheltered harbor. The ship anchored.

"At last!" said Faith. Pounce arched his back, eager to leave the ship.

"Nay, we do stay here to live while the men go ashore to build houses," Faith explained. She sighed. "I fear we must wait a little longer, Pounce. And after coming so far!"

The icy rains of January pounded the ship. Food was running low.

Then the great sickness came.

The Pilgrims were weak from their long journey. They had been cold, wet, and hungry for months. Now, chilly winds blew through the hatches of the ship. People began to cough, their bodies wracked with fever. Then they began to die.

Faith, too, got sick. She lay feverish, her chest sore from coughing. Pounce curled by her tangled hair and would not move.

"Let the mouser stay. He'll do her good," said her father when a leader tried to shoo the cat away.

As Faith drifted in and out of fever, she felt Pounce's soft body against her neck and heard his soothing low purr. When her fever broke, she opened her eyes to Pounce, who had never left her.

By the end of the winter, half the passengers were dead. Those who survived were saddened and frail. The remaining fifty-five Pilgrims moved into seven small houses the men had built.

" 'Tis our new home," Faith told Pounce, carrying him into the house the Barretts would share with others.

At night, in the loft, Faith could hear wolves howling. "I fear the wolves," she said to Pounce. "But mostly, we all fear the Natives. In England, they say these people are savage. I do see them up on the hills, watching us. What are they going to do?"

One March day, a tall Native strode into the little settlement. "Welcome, Englishmen!" he said, in English.

His name was Samoset, and he had learned English from fishermen years ago. Several days later, Samoset returned with his friend, Squanto.

Squanto came to live with the Pilgrims. He, too, spoke English. He helped the Pilgrims make friends with the Native Peoples, who belonged to the Wampanoag tribe. Squanto showed the settlers how to catch eels with their bare hands. He led them to the best thickets for hunting deer. Most important, he taught the Pilgrims how to plant corn, burying two or three herrings along with the corn, then covering kernels and fish with a little hill of earth. The fish would feed the corn, helping it grow tall.

As Faith and the others dug holes, she could see her cat, crouched over the tasty herrings waiting to be buried.

"Shame on thee, Pounce!" she whispered. Quickly, she hid Pounce under her skirts, where she could hear him munching on a stolen fish.

Everyone worked hard that spring. Even Pounce was very busy, catching the chipmunks and squirrels that threatened the crops. He grew strong and fat.

Then, on a night in June, Pounce disappeared.

Three nights, then a week passed, with no Pounce. Faith looked everywhere for him.

Obediently, she milked the goats, fed the chickens, and gathered herbs from her garden. But at night, without Pounce, she cried herself to sleep. When she woke, her eyes were swollen and her cat was still gone.

One day, Squanto led some men to the Eel River to fish. Faith and the other children followed behind. On the way home, Squanto stopped suddenly. He crouched beside a hollow log. Wordless, he beckoned to Faith.

There was Pounce, five tiny kittens snuggling against her!

"Pounce!" exclaimed Faith. She knelt beside her cat. "Thou art a girl! And a mother as well!"

Gently, Squanto lifted Pounce and the kittens and placed them, one by one, in Faith's apron. Faith walked home, apron held high, her eyes fixed on Pounce and her new family.

In the shed behind the Barretts' house, Pounce tended her kittens. As they grew bolder, the kittens ventured into the gardens and fields.

That autumn, the Pilgrims harvested their crops. Fed by the herring, the corn had grown well, with enough to last the coming winter. The beans, squash, and pumpkins had also grown in abundance.

The Pilgrims decided to hold a harvest celebration, much like those they had known back home. Because they were grateful to their Native friends, the Pilgrims invited the Wampanoag.

What a feast was prepared! For days, the men hunted and fished, the women cooked, and the children helped everywhere. Pounce's kittens frolicked underfoot.

One afternoon, as she helped bake cornbread, Faith looked up.
A long file of Wampanoag guests walked into the settlement.
When the Pilgrims greeted their friends, Faith caught a glimpse
of her friend Squanto. She smiled at him.

The most honored Wampanoag and Pilgrims found places inside, while the others gathered at tables set up in the gardens. A Pilgrim leader stood. He thanked God for bringing them safely to this New World, for the rich harvest, and for their new friends, the Wampanoag.

A Wampanoag leader gave thanks to Kietan, Creator of All Things, for the gifts of the ever-bountiful earth.

Then the feast began.

There were roasted turkeys, geese, and deer. There were oysters, cod, and lobsters. There was cornbread. There was squash, beans, corn, and stewed pumpkin. Finally, there were plums, crabapples, dried wild strawberries, and wild grapes.

Faith looked down at her cat, resting at her feet. Worn out by the excitement, the kittens slept beside their mother.

"The *Mayflower* did bring us here safely, Pounce. The Wampanoag are our friends, the harvest is good, and thou hast returned. God be praised!"

Pounce poked her nose from under Faith's skirt. Faith dropped a juicy piece of meat. Pounce crouched. And with great relish, she pounced!

Faith smiled. "Oh, my little mouser! So much to be grateful for!"

From under the table, Pounce purred in agreement.

HUMMELSTOWN COMMUNITY LIBRARY
DAUPHIN COUNTY LIBRARY SYSTEM